for
Elizabeth

STRANGER
K I D S

presents

Printed on recycled paper

First Edition
10 9 8 7 6 5 4 3 2 1

Printed in Hong Kong

Stranger Comics, LLC
4121 Redwood Ave.
Los Angeles, CA 90066

PUBLISHER STRANGER COMICS

PIÑATA IS BASED ON A STORY CREATED BY KEN LOCSMANDI

STRANGERKIDS.COM

Piñata

WRITTEN BY
KEN LOCSMANDI & SEBASTIAN A. JONES

ILLUSTRATED BY
TOMO

PRODUCTION DESIGN BY
CHRISTOPHER GARNER
JEREMY SHUBACK

EDITOR
JOSHUA COZINE

CONCEPT ART BY
TOMO
DARRELL MAY
CLARA JELASSI

ART DIRECTOR
DARRELL MAY

MARKETING
TABITHA GRACE SMITH (CMO)
HANNIBAL TABU (ONLINE)
LEE HAYMORE (US)
SAVAKIS HADJIGEORGIOU (UK)

SPECIAL THANKS
AMAURY NOLASCO
WILMER VALDERRAMA
ERIC FULTON
LLOYD LEVIN
ANDREW COSBY

Upon a warm evening, Jorge was in his old wooden workshop stirring a secret recipe paper mache mix.

Twelve circles to the left and three to the right.

A dash of hope and a sprinkle of light.

Next came the bending of wires and the laying of paper.

He made *piñatas* with joy every day and night.

"Ah, beautiful *chanchito*. You're going to make Lola very happy on her birthday," he beamed, squeezing the pig between the dog and duck.

Plucking his favorite brush, he added the finishing touch.

The duck couldn't contain her excitement. Quick as a wink, her right eye blinked her happy goodbye to her friends!

A brass bell chimed as the door closed behind the old *piñata* maker.

"ALL IS CLEAR!"

was the cheer the *piñatas* barked, squeaked, and howled.

"Lucky ducky!" gasped Miguel, the cheeky monkey.
"I didn't think he was ever gonna finish *gordo* here,"
whined Cynthia, the dog. The newly finished pig didn't feel
chubby. In fact, he felt light and nervously bubbly.

"Yeah, I'm talking about you, Pancho!" she barked.

"My name's Pancho?" whispered the little pig.

"Sure, why not?" added Miguel, unwrapping a banana candy.

"Where did the duck go?" asked Pancho.

To the *piñata fiesta,* of course. It should have been me.

"Listen kid," Miguel offered, "being a *piñata*—"
"Is to be celebrated," interrupted Cynthia. "When you finally
make it to the party, real people lift you up and admire you.
You are the center of attention. Everyone basks in your glory."

"It's every *piñata's* dream, *amigo*. Like a
day in the major leagues," exclaimed Miguel.
"I want to go to the *fiesta*," Pancho squealed politely.

"You're Lola's special *piñata*. You
won't have to wait long," said Miguel.

Cynthia threw her nose up in disgust.
Pancho was a pig, so what was the fuss?

A crescent moon had pierced the gloom outside
Lola's window. The black velvet sky held silver stars high.
They were perfect for dreaming.

"*Abuelo*, does it ever make you sad that the beautiful *piñatas* you make are destroyed?" she asked, most concerned.

"They are never destroyed, Lola. They bring joy to the children and live in our hearts forever," he said, smiling. "Now make your wish and go to sleep."

Lola shut her eyes tight, and with all of her might, made the mightiest wish of all.

The following afternoon, Jorge was preparing
Pancho's tummy for all things yummy.
The little pig was most excited.
Surrounded by a mountain of sweets
and gum drop treats, the *piñata* maker
was determined to make Lola's
birthday one to remember.

Mi chanchito...
do I have a treat for you!

Later that night, when all were still, a light rain tapped on the window sill. A chilly wind crept in.

"Did the old man leave the window open again?" chirped Cynthia, a notoriously light sleeper. "He must know I need my beauty sleep."

She opened her eyes to a sight most fowl, gathered her wits and proceeded to howl...

The duck is COOKED!

Doesn't look like it!" said Miguel.
"It looks like you got attacked
by a dog," which earned him
a swift kick in the butt.

"What happened?"
asked Cynthia.
"It was wonderful. They
recorded it," quacked Donna.
"See for yourself."

"See! Isn't it marvelous?" chimed the chipper duck.

"We gotta bust outta here!" said Miguel, but the window wouldn't budge.

"I feel bloated," oinked Pancho.
"Why would they do this?" asked Cynthia, thinking it was certainly not marvelous.

They want the candy.

Oh, no.

Pancho lay on his belly, which was crammed full of jellies, and waited for his operation. The monkey and dog were eager to perform *piñata* surgery, but the pig had second thoughts.

"Shouldn't it be ladies first, Cynthia?" he squealed feebly.

"You're the chosen one," replied Cynthia with an impish grin, "and you're the only one who's stuffed."

Later, Jorge opened the door, and what he did see, he could not believe. For what he saw was more than before.

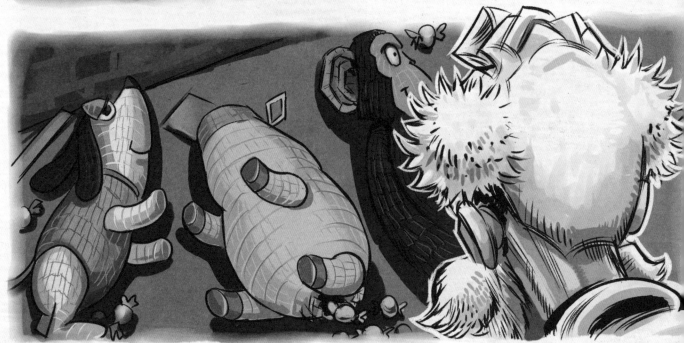

It was a mess! More or less. The *piñatas* kept quiet as mice.

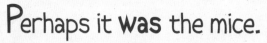Perhaps it **was** the mice.

They were known taffy takers and gobstopper robbers.

"I'll have to deal with this jumble later," he mumbled,

scooping up the once portly pig.

"We must fill you up again and

get to Lola's *fiesta*."

It was midday when the hip hip hoorays were about to get underway. Hoisting Pancho into the air, the maker and pig started to stare into each other's eyes. When they were nose to nose, Jorge said, "You'll make *Lolita* so happy, *mi amigo.*" With that, the old man went inside the house.

Pancho had other ideas.

With a wiggle and a tuggle, as fast as he could struggle, the piggle unraveled his rope. He was free! THUD!

After landing on his tush, he made for the bush, as quick as his little legs would carry him. It was the perfect hiding spot.

Then out came the kids with wonder and glee. Wearing hats and wielding bats, they were ready for festivities.

But the smiles turned down to droopy frowns when they saw the pig had gone.

Sitting in her most beautiful birthday dress, Lola asked...

"Ay no, it was just here," he said. "Perhaps it was the candy thieves?"

"It's okay, *Abuelo*. Let's go back inside," said Lola bravely.

Pancho watched them enter the house. "Oh, what a muddle," oinked the pig in a puddle. Now he could run for freedom, he thought, wiping a tear from his eye. But why was he blubbering?

With a big hearty sigh, he realized why, and stepped on out of the shrubbery.

That got everyone's attention, and soon the door swung open. Jorge stood in amazement with Lola smiling brightly for all to see. Pancho was back. *"Gracias, chanchito!"* she said.

The moon started to climb. It was clean up time as Jorge gathered pieces of Pancho. Legs in one hand and head in the other, it was no wonder Lola looked down so.

Abuelo, why are you throwing away my beautiful *chanchito*?

"It is no good anymore," he replied.
Jorge looked at Pancho and then to his Lola, and remembered
the gift that is a *piñata*! They live in our hearts forever!

You are right.
It is beautiful...

"...and perfect the way it is."

The *fiesta* was over, but all would remember
a most magical day on the tenth of November.

The End

Xavi

Xavi is the secret king of the sweet little thieves. He teaches candy karate at *piñata* parties to all the mice, whether naughty or nice, who yearn to learn the secret arts of stealing tarts!

Big D

Big D is a mouse that munches morning, noon, and night.
Wearing edible aprons, he tops red velvet cakes with raspberry
jelly beans whenever he bakes!

Go

Go is the gummy glue that holds the crew together. He is very fond of swimming in ponds of soda pop with lemon drops and rowing cupcakes across milkshake lakes!

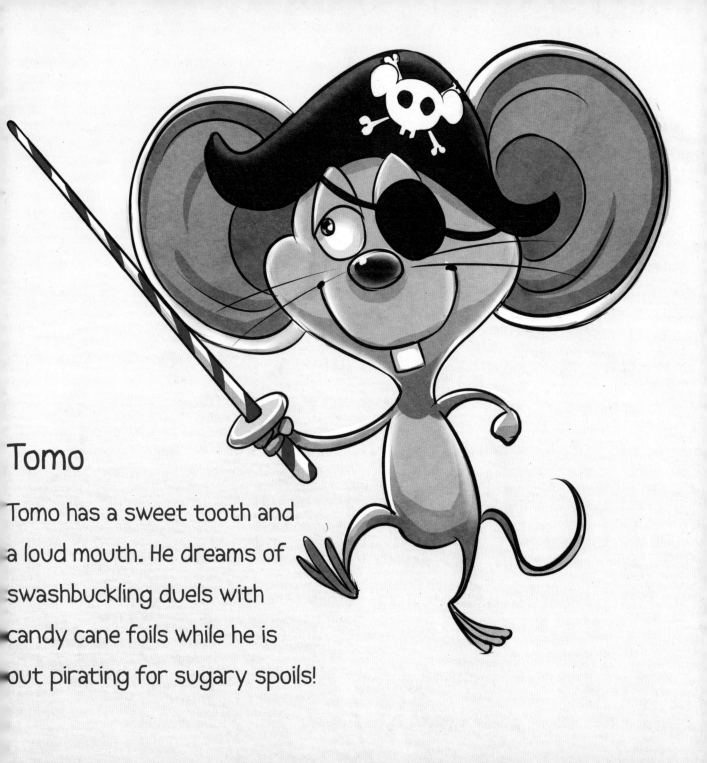

Tomo

Tomo has a sweet tooth and a loud mouth. He dreams of swashbuckling duels with candy cane foils while he is out pirating for sugary spoils!

Yosh

Yosh is a charmer, dreamer, and wishful thinker.

He is quiet when others are loud.

He is humble when others are proud.

Yosh is the heart and soul of the rodent rogues!

STRANGER
K I D S

presents

Want to Make a *Piñata* like Pancho?

Ingredients

I Round Balloon

2 oz of White School Glue
(about half of a bottle)

I Large Bowl

A Stack of Old Newspapers

A Pair of Scissors

Non-Toxic or Poster Paint

Colored Crepe Paper or
Crepe Party Streamers

I Safety Pin

3 Toilet Paper Rolls

I Pink Fuzzy Pipe Cleaner

Step 1

Blow up a round balloon. The size of your balloon is the size of your pig's body.

Step 2

Mix 2 ounces of glue
with 3 cups of water
in a large bowl.

Step 3

Tear or cut newspapers into strips.

Step 4

Dip a strip of newspaper into the glue. Stick the strips on the balloon.
Cover the balloon with 4 layers of newspaper strips. Don't cover the
end where the balloon tie is (the bottom of your *piñata*).

Step 5

Let the balloon dry (usually overnight)

Step 6

Cut 2 toilet paper rolls in half.

Try to make them the same size.

These are Pancho's feet.

Glue them to the bottom of your *piñata*. Cut another toilet paper roll so it's about 2 inches wide. This is Pancho's nose.

Glue that to the side of your *piñata*. Wait for everything to dry.

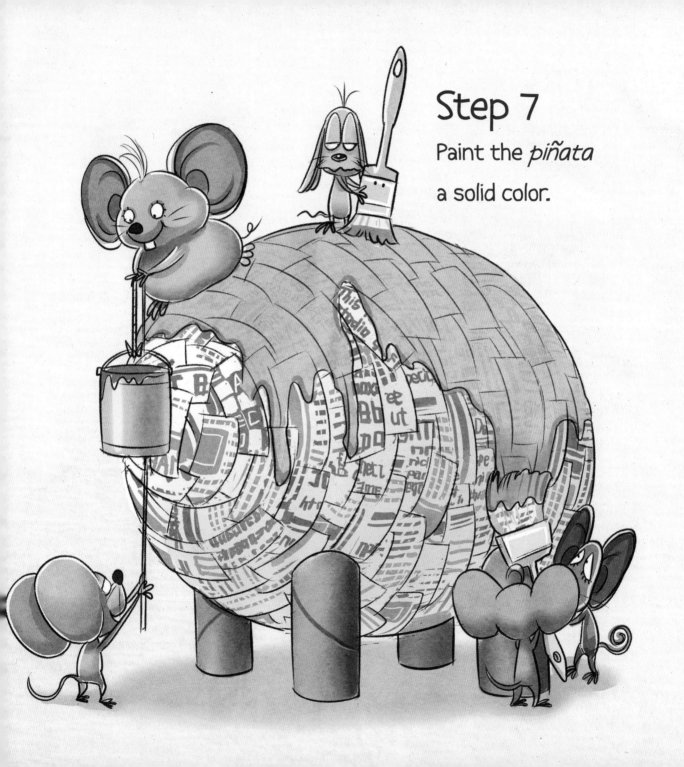

Step 7

Paint the *piñata*

a solid color.

Step 8

Cut crepe paper or streamers into strips. You can cut a fringe along one edge. You can use all one color or lots of colors.

Stick the strips in rows along your *piñata*.

Cover Pancho's feet and snout with crepe paper too.

Step 9

Pop the balloon with a safety pin!

Step 10

Take one fuzzy pipe cleaner and wrap it around your finger so it looks like a twisty pig tail.

Gently push one end of the tail into the back of your *piñata*. Optionally, you can use a ribbon as his tail, or you can tie a ribbon around his tummy like Lola did.

Step 11

Trace out the template for
Pancho's eyes, ears, and nose
on a new sheet of paper.
Then color them and cut them out.
Fold the ears along the tab and glue
the tab to the *piñata* so his ears
stand up straight.

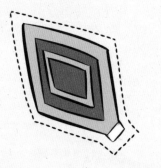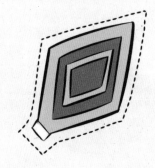

las orejas

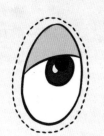

los ojos

la nariz

Step 12

Stuff your *piñata* with candy!

Use masking tape to cover up the hole when you're done.

Step 13
Enjoy!